We're going on an ELF CHASE

Words by
Martha Mumford

Illustrated by
Laura Hughes

BLOOMSBURY
CHILDREN'S BOOKS
LONDON OXFORD NEW YORK NEW DELHI SYDNEY

We're going on an elf chase.

Come and join the fun.

Can we catch them all?

YES!
Run, run, run!

We're going on an elf chase.
Flip, flap, slide.
Watch out for the
PENGUINS...

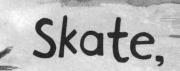

Skate,

skate,

glide!

We're going on an elf chase.

Come and join the fun.

Can we catch them all?

YES!
Run, run, run!

We're going on an elf chase.

Chirpy, chirpy, cheep.

Watch out for the

ROBINS...

Tippy-toe,

creep!

We're going on an elf chase.

Come and join the fun.

Can we catch them all?

YES!
Run, run, run!

We're going on an elf chase.

Zzzz, zzzz, snore.

Watch out for the

POLAR BEARS...

Don't
make
them
roar!

North Pole →

We're going on an elf chase.

Come and join the fun.

Can we catch them all?

YES!
Run, run, run!

We're going on an elf chase.

Slippety, slip, slip.

Watch out for the

REINDEER ...

Cloppy, cloppy, clip!

We're going on an elf chase.

Come and join the fun.

Can we catch them all?

YES!
Run, run, run!

Quick, quick, reindeer –

Cloppy, cloppy, clip!

Quick, quick, bears –

Grrr, grrr, roar!

Quick, quick, robins –

Chirpy, chirpy, cheep!

Quick, quick, penguins –

Flip, flap, slide!

Quick, quick, little buns – *run, run, run ...*

Everyone off to sleep.
Shh, now close your eyes.
When you wake up
in the morning . . .